poems of adventure

a selection of poems

EDITED BY JESSICA CLARK AND
STEPHANIE HANSON

Notice of Copyright

Amazon KDP. Available from Amazon and other retail outlets

ISBN 979-8-5647-3120-1

Dedication

For Kevin Griffin, a contributor who sadly passed away this year.

And to all who have suffered a loss in one way or another this year.

Table of contents

Foreword..11

setting out..14

Emerge...16
Katie Mcevoy
Forever...16
Tatiana Khalyako
Wait for Me...17
Jessica Clark
A story about a boat-trip.....................................18
Richard W. Halperin
Prelude..22
Janet Butler
Childhood...23

Particular...26
Ruby McCann
Ode to a Latin Stranger.....................................26
Stephanie Hanson
Heat..30
Obinna Chilekezi
I have to leave (a poem)....................................31
Asha Sumroy

Desert Sun..32

Sense..35

Josh Newmark
Peace..35
Jennifer Carr
In this Moment..36
Rose Proudfoot
Froglet..36
Bruach Mhor
In my top pocket—all the way..37
John Carew
The Atlas..38

Arise..40

Jennifer Carr
My Sanctuary..40
Cameron Bramley
Desert Rose..41
Jennifer Carr
A Prayer for My Owl Spirit..41
Jakey Zee
Choose Life..42
Janet Butler
Vanishing Point..44

the journey..46

Moments 48

Abi Brown
Torrent 48
Darren Donohue
Wanderlust 50
Bill Cushing
At a Mountain Waterfall 51
Richard Smith
A New Dawn 53
Paul Robert Mullen
the journey 55
Cameron Bramley
Dive into Darkness 57

Destinations 60

David Del Mundo
Barcafoba 60
Anne Hornsby
Venice 61
Daniel Mercieca
Falcon 63
Stephanie Hanson
Plaza de Oriente 64
Veronica Aaronson
Leaving Iona – North Beach 66
Darren Donohue
Postcard 68

Memories 71

Paul W. Byrne
Fealeings...71
Jessica Clark
Snow...76
Alison Liew
How Normal Feels Like..............................78
Peter Donelly
Devon in my nineteenth year.....................80

Motion...83

Norbert Góra
This is how the journey looks like................83
Darren Donohue
Grace..84
James Swansbrough
Remember When......................................86
Zoe Ellesmore
Driving, on the South Circular...................88
Nathanael O'Reilly
Reprieve..90
Bernadette Jameson
Traffic Flow...92

Reflections..95

John Carew
Tonight is for my Odyssey.........................95
Niamh O 'Meara
Reminiscence..99
Kat Dyb

Time Zones..100
Ruby McCann
I'm still considering.................................101
Jen Nolan
Rest..105
Jessica Clark
Days of yore..107
Ella Taylor
The Redwoods...108

homecoming...111

Amber..112

Anne Hornsby
The Wanderer's Return............................112
Ruby McCann
Homespun..114
Anne Hornsby
Coming Home...116

Expanse..119

Geno Naughton
Robinsonade..119
Ross Walsh
An Galar Mór...120

Converge..122

Stephanie Hanson
Old Town...122
Danielle Silverman
Snout of the Year.....................................124
Kevin Griffin
What the Wall Said..................................126
Holly Parkinson
St. John's Street.......................................127
Elijah MacBean
Bridge..128

Hollow...131

Aldo Quagliotti
Meta-morphosis.....................................131
Asha Sumroy
Meditations on an Empty House..............132
Danielle Silverman
Tory Cave..136
Jessica Clark
Cleaning out the fridge...........................139
Pete Chambers
Nearly There..141

Cool..144

Obinna Chilekezi
Early Morning Rain...............................144
Alice Carlill
saltwater...145
Harry Mizumoto

a complex system of weights and pulleys...148
Cameron Bramley
Shimmer..148
Gareth Writer-Davies
Here..150

Acknowledgment and Credits...152

Foreword

2020 has seen us move from a moment in history when more widespread travel was permitted to restrictions across much of the world - that have kept us on a leash from our front doors, or in some cases, stuck behind them. At a time where physical movement is limited, the use of imagination to connect with diverse spaces and experiences enhancing human life seems paramount.

As fellow seekers of adventure, we both feel intimately connected to the allure of the "quest" – its challenges, thrills, and the potential it has to open individuals up to the possibilities of endless curiosity and the exploration. Both of us have chosen to feed our wanderlust in myriad ways: be that through living abroad in a hostel, where friendships burgeoned and awe-inspiring stories were told on an hourly basis, or hitching a taxi with strangers met abroad and sharing woes, sins and aspirations in ill-advised detail, dancing and crying, all in the flash of a hot summer's night.

While 2020 has rendered this form of travel remote, it has also taken backpacking-enamoured generations on a new journey - into domestic spheres and inner stores of resilience. From the surge in poetry and artistic practice taking during the COVID-19 lockdowns, it is abundantly clear that creative expression continues to represent a lifeline and indispensable pathway into discovering ourselves and our world.

Hence, inasmuch as this anthology brings together poets whose words allow for exploration beyond isolation's walls, this collection aims to offers something dynamic, expansive even, at a time where societies are vulnerable to stagnation. Our intention is that this anthology will take you on a journey traversing not only cultural and spatial boundaries but also metaphorical roads through memory, healing, loss and emotion.

We thank profoundly our contributors, without whom this tribute to Earth's nooks and crannies would not be possible. Sincere thanks also to the talented artists Christine Butler and Joan Fullerton, whose dazzling creations bring to light these pages. While not quite matching the length of *The Odyssey*, *Poems of Adventure* has become somewhat longer than initially anticipated! That being said, there is not a single poem that we do not consider integral to the jigsaw of words and experiences this anthology brings together.

We have both found solace in exploring our passion for creative writing nurtured over the course of our time studying at Durham University, and following our first anthology *Poems of Hope*, centred around the theme of mental health, we couldn't have set upon a better venture to embark upon.

> *Continent, city, country, society:*
> *the choice is never wide and never free.*
> *And here, or there... No. Should we have stayed at*
> *home,*
> *wherever that may be?*

Elizabeth Bishop

Questions of Travel

Many thanks and merry reading,

Jess and Stephanie

setting out

Emerge

Katie Mcevoy

Forever

The mountains are my cage

Framing the horizon in all directions

They contain me

In this place where time is measured by the falling leaves,

Days are counted by the flower of the cane

Where I find myself awake

After a sleep resembling an eternity

The rain stirred me

With its cold touch, the world gently shook me

And as my eyes opened to see

The sun's rays shone upon my skin

Where once the bars had been

Now the mountains framed - not a prison

But a whisper of possibility

They spoke to me of endless opportunities

They spoke to me of forever.

Tatiana Khalyako

Wait for Me

Belonging to no one and nowhere

I wrote a lonely freedom

Just for me

Selfishly thieved stars

And grasped at sunsets

Kissed snowflakes, inhaled the rain

Wanting to know everything someday

Always on the run from nothing and no one

I halted
In the haze
Foreshadowing sleep.
For a moment there were we
Sensing privacy

I left the woozy morning
With dewy darkness
Dripping from its lashes
The night no more
Than a ripple on my mind

I'm moving on
I'm no longer scared
Still free, I know
Someone is waiting for me
Somewhere

Jessica Clark

A story about a boat-trip

Darkness

flowing from a nib

in the sanctuary of a bedroom

in the middle of an evening;

Ink spills onto nothingness

and blank white becomes words

so from nowhere blooms this story,

this nonsense, gibberish,

arbitrary shapes with all this power –

letters –

and that blank black thread

spills to a river instead

winding through fields towards a shoreline

words cloying their cobwebs

weaving and sticking to an erected image of two fig-
ures

and building the path for the vessel they climb onto,

building the vessel,

and building the motion of climbing....

Through the reader's eye

alighting on which book to choose

and thumbing its pages, leafing through

eyes resting on one deemed suitable
and from their gaze springs the story
light waves hitting the back of retina,
picture flipped upside down
and characters processed.

Between the oar and the water
of a rowing boat gliding towards high tide
where the sunset shines vermilion across the sky
and a pair of unknowing passengers ride
innocently spinning narrative as they steer their way
moving past fields in the closing day –
a little conversation, but mainly silence –
some musing on the path
at a steady point in the journey:
a mission mentioned many times,
but for now, just river's rhythmic lines,
the smell of harvest mixed with brine,
dusky stillness, flat flowering landscape,
and a reaching hand to touch the other's arm.
Precipice of calm
shared by two
while the embers of red light

grow ready to melt into stars

and the cross-marked points of a map

point forwards, like a mirror to the night.

It starts with two people

boarding a boat

which rocks a little to take their weight

or does it start with an impulse to create?

Or was it as I wrote that this was born?

Or your thumbing of the page?

Or the story blooming in your head?

Or even in some part of the future? –

When it's replayed quite by mistake

unanticipated in a quiet moment,

notes rising from nowhere onto the stave of memory

in my mind or in yours –

or in some long-off notion of the journey

a universal spirit haunting moulds of verse and prose –

from there it grows,

the shaking and shaping of oars,

dark waters lapping at the first splash of creation.

Richard W. Halperin

Prelude

Let us go to Ethiopia, my dear,

Let us pry the possible out of the jam jar.

Let us think of Jesus, if that is not too painful.

Let us think of golden things in the form of words.

A good cup of Moka Java, pronounced

    as W.C. Fields pronounced it

Would not be out of place.

I am not sure

You are willing to go with me

Back there where we once were

But since everything which ever happened

Or is happening

Or ever will happen

Is stuck where it is in thie gum of time

We are together in Addis

Without the trouble and expense

    of another voyage

Because und so weiter.

The expectation, which any child has,

That a word on its way to being uttered

Will turn out to be better than what it turns out to be

Keeps us going.

Twenty-three people since the world began

Fulfilled that hope

And there their books still are,

Ignored by the glittering stampede of the hysterical.

Of those so desperate for wisdom

That they never rest

Never breathe on two or three words

Since words are mayflies

In the golden light

Which fly delicately and mate and die

Almost invisibly

In Sligo in Addis and points west.

Janet Butler

Childhood

Sun touched everything then

Sky blues muted to whites, a shimmering halo
around that golden globe, the center of our universe.
It swelled summer to high colors
green leaves gleamed and cast a flutter of bird shadows,
cool and secretive beneath strong limbs
closed to tender us.

We became flickering fish in brown river waters
wild flowers sprouting along dirt paths we followed
to fresh mysteries in dense woods.
We chased that arch of sun and folded at dusk
buds tight in dreams suckled yet by Gaia.

POOL OF LIGHT © *JOAN FULLER-TON*

Particular

Ruby McCann

Ode to a Latin Stranger

(1639 Monroe Street, NW, Washington, DC)

beginnings..,

...so pleased to hear you
I like bright and dark sounds
that saxophone   screams

something lonesome

I'm new here
re-new-ed   been before
was born here   re-turn-er
it's like locking a woman in a room
with an angry man

feels alright   now
in this moment...
...he's on the right side of angry
lonely won't leave him alone
and this place stinks to high heavens
doesn't that tell you something?

don't know what's ahead
I've lost my sea legs
yes   the ocean   I'm here
at the Firth of Clyde
flowing into the Atlantic
to you   my dear friend
on the other side
its daunting sometimes

the vast infinite width
and depth   the divide

other times
it un-anchors me
takes me down deep within
a-minor tsunami at low tide

calms too   calming   yes
yes   calm as the day
Icarus fell chasing dreams

was he fallen?   did he fall?
smashed against a rock
I heard   seas
unpredictable like that
a sudden change in weather
raging surfs slap like angry parents
my mother   once
not my father   shocked me
she cried afterwards   empty-eyed
like a ghost in the kitchen

me too   silently

alone in the bathroom

knowing   I deserved it

I know these are small things

just coasting   not just

still there are days I feel I can't be fussed

I know I need to re-adjust

re-learn to trust

get real   or completely combust

then I turn like tides

today the flow can't wait

cause it's so good to hear from you

whitecaps rolling in

my lips curling   a-drifting smile

softening   splaying

foaming high-pitched

strains on that horn   whispering

s'bin too long

I catch you on the high note

I'm switched on   enriched

screaming staccato   you got me bewitched

releasing water keys

it's been a long session

sliding cross rhythms

my trans-Atlantic connection

Stephanie Hanson

Heat

Two heavy bodies, bleary from the books, raise each other to a task

The words will wait, the scores will be as they have always been,

Now is to escape the life-cage that enfolds us -

To enter into reckless misadventure

To roam 'al fresco' in the grand outdoors.

Letters scribbled into pages

Cast away and loosely flung

As this pair of hopeful vagabonds

Crept out and out and, and pensively at first,

Latched onto the ground beneath them

One by one,

Rubbing sandals clamoured and took flight

Pummelled down the road, through backstreet lanes,

By valleyed shops, the county pubs

A cottage with its chimney, gently fuming

Launched into the steep below

Where a scrubbed out path with hedges overgrown
broke through unto the open sky

Out by the green.

It takes two to wander

In the heat

To a field of Bluebells

For we were promised Bluebells

Out where a string of marbled trees caress the Wear's
unending curves,

Where a Willow willfully lays bear its weighty
branches

Out where the Wood adorns her warm, damp beds with
a blowing, cobalt shock.

Obinna Chilekezi

I have to leave (a poem)

A fine Sunday morning
A bird and his mate at my window
Singing songs of love together.
This country is
Full of pretty feathers
And aviary songs -
I love her
But the taxi's outside
Waiting, and I have to leave
These songs, these feathers and her tears

Asha Sumroy

Desert Sun

I bought new shampoo because it promised
highlights like the desert sun
Still, I will never yearn for anything like sand
In the soft skin innocence
On the base of my feet

Or euphoria rain on the stone of a
Jerusalem rooftop—seeping through clothes and
Through words

The sky in London is beautiful but painted
into a perpetual state of clouded longing -
It knows across continents
there's a deeper blue
And the pavements here sing of grazed
knees in magical years
But not of hope or home

I miss the hope in the stones

And accidentally swallowing the gritty
last mouthful of Turkish coffee that that same waiter
never minds if I can't find the change for—granules in
teeth like sand in feet and tobacco caught in the seams
of borrowed clothes—lingering remnants of the dusks
and dawns that formed the start of the rest of our
lives

I miss the gaps
between buildings that became our favourite shortcuts

© *CHRISTINE BUTLER*

Sense

Josh Newmark

Peace

Half city and half hill

Where the barrios tumble down from Alto

Until it's hard to tell which way is up

It's cold and a little bleak, in places

But you're never far from colour

Nor from a cable car to lift you above everything

So drink your coca tea and beware breathtaking views

There's little breath to spare at 12,000 feet

Jennifer Carr

In this Moment

I wait and hold my breath
For the movement of wings—the sky beckoned and insisted
I soar where angels sing
following destiny's trail
riding on a hawk's tail
Looking through my telescopic eye
I defy all odds the higher I fly
Waiting for the wind to stroke my face

Rose Proudfoot

Froglet

bisexual began
in the tiny black pupil of a frogspawn pearl.

it grew inside a jellied eye.
shuddering out a tail, feathered gills.

dilating as it observed a dim world.
sucking in light light a vacuum.

it collapsed on itself, reforming.
nudging through slime into water.

it swam, distilling oxygen
from the pond like an alchemist.

conjuring itself four legs, feet.
absorbing its tail.

then it surfaced. head plunging
into air. blinking, born again.

flat ribbons of lung expanding.
breathing, for the very first time.

Bruach   Mhor

In my top pocket—all the way

What would I carry?

A flat periwinkle from home

always the perfect shade

"Sir", I'd offer,
"here is the exact colour –
just what you need"

or "Madam, consider this..."
showing the shell
in my open palm.

No guarantee of anything
no certainty
only enchantment.

John Carew

The Atlas

Hung imprisoned in its timber casing
on the wall above the blackboard
The Master would pull the string
and like a blind, it would lower
shutting out the darkness from all our minds
And there, like magic in front of our very eyes
the world in all its greatness
Vast oceans deep blue
the deeper the ocean the deeper the blue

Broad mountains, dark brown
the higher the mountain the darker the brown
Great cities, a blood red dot
the greater the city the larger the dot
With his rod, which often burnt our flesh
He would randomly point to the atlas
"name the country-"
"Egypt Sir."
"and its capital-"
"Cairo Sir."
The Master would be in his element
"Close your eyes and feel the bustle of the crowded
streets,
Smell the aromatic spices from a trader's stalls
Walk through Tahrir Square and peer into
Egyptian Museums,
trove of antiquities, of royal mummies,
of gilded artefacts and of King Tutankhamun
Sail down the crocodile-infested Nile
Wonder at the magnitude of the Pyramids,
burial place to the Pharaohs of Egypt."

Arise

Jennifer Carr

My Sanctuary

She no longer has a hold on me
My soul has finally learned to transcend
both time and space

I rise above the birds
Charting beyond the clouds
Clarity surrounds me in the skies
Anxiety no longer consumes
my chakras

The sky is my sanctuary
In peace, in prayer
I fly away

Cameron Bramley

Desert Rose

Windswept and widowed by the stark, dry faintedness of another's heart. The cover against the blizzard of dusted parts of yourself is lifting with the winds of change. Your spirit is a rose— water it, with the morning dew, grow into the colour hidden. Reach into the sky and touch the silver cloud you so often know is there. And when you touch it, remember it. For you are your own magic, your own rainbow.

Jennifer Carr

A Prayer for My Owl Spirit

If I were I born a mighty bird
I would soar over mountains
Look to the moon for direction
for an unseen spirit

with unknown powers,
eyes that see through the darkest hour.

The moon, glowing. Above the treeline
outshining shadows lurking
among the wonder of the stars—
even as the fullness of the moon fades

Spirit, grace my wings
with freedom

whether travelling near or far
let your presence be known
so I may never be alone

Jakey Zee

Choose Life

Choose Life, choose a normal life, be a grey believer,
business as usual, got to work, got to get a job and fit
into a system that will bring us all to our knees, get a
car, scroll through endless newsfeeds. Turn a blind eye
to your inner treasures, lose yourself in TV, sort out

your debts, paperwork, fines, credit card bills and order that gizmo online. Make a couple of phone calls, have an anxiety moment when your Spirit briefly surfaces. Counter it with complexes and guilt, wonder if it was always like this? Analyse your complicity in it all, and plan a way out of the debilitating slavery. Book your doctors appointment, take your medication, buy a new microwave and pick up some of those energy saving, mercury filled cancer causing light bulbs. Chase your ex, chase your past, reflect on all the things that didn't last, go on Twitter, bang one out, remember the days of Twist And Shout. Play the game, stare into space, reflect on all the fucking waste. Plastic bottles fill our shores, better recycle a little bit more... Ease your conscience with a plan, but end up back on Instagram. Go to London for the day, pretend to make the System pay, believe that you can change the world, make a better place for the boys and girls. Subscribe to another YouTube channel, and watch an hour or two of flannel. Look out the window what you see, the slaughtered remains of a row of trees. A glossy leaflet drops through your door, reminding you to spend even more. Another one follows about 5G, promoting Skynet technology, that will cook you all inside your homes, but with quicker downloads you'll never be alone. Refuse to play the System's game, and enjoy the freedom that you'll gain, by being real to the core, and give up the idea of consuming more. Dare to be happy for the entire day, open your heart and allow it to say, express those thoughts you keep inside and bloody well have a sense of pride. You made it mate, have a herbal tea, while a chem-trail line slips silently, across the sky with its toxic spread, just don't give up, don't stay in bed.... It's all ok, we will prevail, just burn all copies of the Daily Mail. You have to live your life, they say, so be brave.... And make it start to-day....

Janet Butler

Vanishing Point

All roads lead to Rome.
Perhaps not.

I posit:
a rough grained paper stretched taut
a gliding pencil
meeting resistance.

Minuscule ridges and valleys that pull and break
then smooth soft graphite
into paths a stop start pause then push.
A pioneer through virgin lands.

Lines connect and curves enclose
and angled corners promise depths
distant hills cover distant hills,
all vanishing at that still point
where all roads lead.

the journey

Moments

Abi Brown

Torrent

I am sat,

On the back of his bike,

And we are blinded by rain.

I have always loved,

The damp,

Afternoon petricor

But I have never felt a downpour,

Like this.

We keep the engine

Ticking over,

Restless in the flood.

This rain is warm

Heavy like

A long breath,

In a strange place.

Baptised by this torrent

Perhaps - take

our sins,

Before they have time,

To wash us both away.

I am clean in this rain

Thrown through a monsoon,

Protests drowned

In Holy Water.

For a God, I feel,

Has his hands on me;

Turning over, restive,

roaring, endless;

never telling,

what he has in store for me.

Darren Donohue

Wanderlust

I enter the train toilet
to wash my hands
but a plant commandeers the sink,

it sprouts from the washbasin,
spreading its branches
through the open window.

In hot pursuit
of this leafy mystery,
I strip to the waist,

smear my chest with soap
and squeeze through the tiny opening.
A forest flowers on each carriage top,

forming a whipping tail
of loose roots, wagging the train
under bridges and through towns.

Each flower, shrub, and bush

racing away breathless,

shaking off the soil that anchors.

Bill Cushing

At a Mountain Waterfall

water slaps my face

forcing my eyes

shut

as we climb crablike,

scuttling from

    platform

       to platform

    along the rocks

that form   an opening

not more than a half-foot across

       and from that six-inch aperture

     water shoots

       out

       and

       down

rocks run

in steps.
vines crawl
down
and—nourished by the trickling water that
splashes
runs
pounds
and
flows—
begin to take root
on
another
base of rock

holding a stone shaped
like an axe
as big as my hand,
as thick
and
almost as flat
except for one hard wart at
the broader end

other men
there might have been
here using rocks

like this one
chipping them into tools
and weapons
on this island—
into all things
primitive

Richard Smith

A New Dawn

Pre-Dawn mist,
Suspended,
Still,
Resembling an eerie Spectre,
Shrouding Lake from hidden Hills.

Pale Halo to the east,
Begins to advance on the dark foe of night,
As triumphant hills are liberated,
By Dawns rising light.

Unnerving hoots of Owls,
a test of my will,
Are mellowed by chirping,

That soon overspills.

Mists now dispersed.

Chilled vapour gone,

Having fleetingly changed its visage,

Before conceding to the Morn.

The first Beam of Sun,

Reveals Webs embellished with Dew,

They quiver and float by my spirit,

Finally peaceful and soothe.

My Pew,

A fallen Oak,

Dethroned,

Yet even still,

Embodied in a regal Tapestry,

Being woven by Nature's wondrous will.

A glance exchanged - startles a curious Frog,

Prompting its plunge into the placid waters chill,

Captivated,

I watched the ripples dissipate and,

With time,

I see it still.

I witness an early morning Bee,

Devoted,

Ahead of any queue,

Understand the quest for Nectar,

While certain,

It soon would find it too...

Paul Robert Mullen

the journey

the journey has changed

today i wander to the bathroom

lather & rinse at my own pace

bathe the sleep from shadow stained eyes

brush fuzzy teeth without urgency

there is no clock holding

my ransom

today i amble downstairs into the silence

where otherwise the scitter-scatter of rushing
    feet would clatter

take rest upon a bar stool at the

kitchen counter // watch the kettle steam

and chortle

smooth butter onto crumpets asif

stroking a canvas

today i mosey into the garden

within my castle walls

set up with coffee // book // laptop

under gazebo shade
    watch the queen bee peruse

the warming spring delights

let the minutes drain steadily into afternoon

today i retire to the living room

nuzzle with the dog in front of Netflix

feet elevated on the armrest

a dash of rijoca // home-cooked korma

watch the barren street slide
    seductively for dusk

the city is already a memory
a fond one at that –
   the buzz of train platforms
rustle of bags // voices // car exhausts
and common goodbyes
     somewhere to be

midnight arrives
like any other double-fingered milestone

i check the menu
   pick out another unfamiliar horror
PLAY

Cameron Bramley

Dive into Darkness

As I stand on the cliff
Ready with my bag full of parachute
Below swirls the darkness
waves breaking on the shores of my mind
My feet leave the ground

I dive

The air smacks my body as it hurtles down
Turning to wind, it wraps around my skin
Light fades, dim dusty middle dark flies by
into darkness

Liquid black covers me
Feels like the ooze,
The placenta of a new birth
Into more light and more shine
One with beauty and bounty

Crawling to the shores of the changed me
Boldly I walked to
where light is liquid and darkness has its rightful
place

I stand on the cliffs of my life again
If jumping is freedom
Then let me jump

© *C H R I S T I N E   B U T L E R*

Destinations

David Del Mundo

Barcafoba

A million different faces
A hundred different encounters
Of very little value
  - Fake opinions buying attention
Good vibes
Good amigos
Then, nada.
  - Flaking on me again
Free entry into whositswhats
  - Falling over broken arrangements

Come on in, we'll give you all free shots

    - Finding old bruises again

Ya know, trust is a tricky thing to tackle

    - Friction over bullshit actions

Especially when people only love you for your tobacco

    - From over bearing acquaintances

Las Ramblas is a fucking toilet

    - Finding other broken amigos

You go to tie your shoe laces, yet no one waits

You offer a smile, yet they look to the ground

You think you're living, yet it's just killing time

    - Feeling only better afterwards

Why stick around, when there's something better. Is the grass always greener on the other side?

    - Fear of being anonymous

    - Fear of being alone

Benvinguts a Barcefoba

A n n e   H o r n s b y

V e n i c e

The sun slowly crept higher

Unfurled pink fingers
as I blinked up at the Mediterranean sky,
Winced slightly as I shifted my weight
On the unforgiving hardness of the
station platform
Uncurled my back.
Tilted back my head.
I read the sign above:
Venice it said:
City of romance
City of dreams
of canals and bridges
of back-packing tourists, it seems.
In their sleeping bags
Lying in rows
Ready to be woken.

Explore.
To do.
At one.
with this ancient, floating, water-locked city.
Then onwards
More

Travelling

More

Journeying

More

Trains

More.

Daniel Mercieca

Falcon

Driving down to Devon
Past waves of rolling hills and tides of
trees,
Desiring, as waves of
old Stonehenge past,
To be out of the smog and in the sea.

Falcon is a place of mental flight,
Sitting still as cliffs both smile and scowl
Across the countless days
and cloudless nights
a shrine of solitude, perched next to Owl.

We often wander through the cliffs to Beer,
Quenching our thirst high at the Fountain's Head
with folk rock, hog roasts and with busy cheer;
Or we embrace the Mason's Arms instead.

Beach-combing at Branscombe;
Running my eyes through pebbles like pages
Of a story, seeking blown and handspun
caressive waves that stroke the ages.
A mosaic of bottle-green, seafoam and
pearl
At the bottom of Castle Rock is scattered;
worth more to me than any coins we hurl
around in cities with ceilings to be
shattered.

To live on the edge is to sit by the sea,
Where time runs slow, and feelings soar.

Stephanie Hanson

Plaza de Oriente

To a not so quiet spot, where majestic and irreverent seems

That rampant chatter, those broad, bright lungs and snazzy sounds

That fill the leafy stage with plumes of sentimental pleasure.

The prima donna blasts the senses, growing through dynamic lines that playfully suffuse the ground's surroundings

Guests gather on broad walkways or

Drink to the views from hotel balconies as

Gardens and gilded arches of the palace illustriously sing.

Outdoor tables, chairs – cafés all lined with blooming parasols shade the sitters-in

While long-found lovers lean into their toasts, to leisure and to liberty

The Plaza de Oriente

Where even strangers meet a loudness felt so large,

A sensibility so strong

All reticence gives way, instantaneously, to fancy and delight

Where rows or aromatic flowers circling Felipe and the
fourty-four
Enrapture and excite

Dear Isabel, safely I can report that even now
Wine spills over green into tall glasses,
And lulls the easy traveller into a woozy trance,
As the gifts of your sovereignty interminably repour

Veronica Aaronson

Leaving Iona – North Beach

Wanting to eke out its last gifts before I'm
ferried back to where
I call home,

I undress my feet, soak up the warmth as
one might absorb the heat of a lover's
flat, warm palm.

Take in the salty air, the sound of lulling waves,
the slight give of ground under
my weight

step around the driftwood, channelled wrack, knotted
kelp,
the bones of something
I cannot seem to name.

And something, that might or might not be me,
unearthing untold stories held
between my breaths.

That this dialogue might never be again,
stings the backs of my eyes,
births a yearning.

I pocket a pebble - not of a serpentine green
but of a selkie grey, the shape
and size of a single eye,

and leave the imprint of my raw heels
splayed toes - a map
of my brief passing.

Although migrations will

come between us, I know I will not stop
returning.

Darren Donohue
Postcard.

Can the church bells of Nice heal me?
I stand by her castle gates, deciphering
patterns in the sea. They creep forward,
tumbling over the lightest blue.

A holy procession appears from an alley,
the priest four-cornered beneath a red canopy.
He's singing with the faithful,

their hymn washing over the cobblestones,
children throw rose petals to sweeten the air,
their parents moving in-step, clutching their bibles.
But before I can ask for the right prayer,
they vanish through a glowering arch.
With eyes shut, I swim out between corridors
of melting waves. Hungry for release,
clawing the shore, they spin me around

like the hand on a compass.

DIMENSIONS OF AIR © JOAN FULLERTON

Memories

Paul W. Byrne

Fealeings

All night he visualized the moment

Awakening, he slipped softly from the bedroom

Creeping downstairs in the darkness

Feeling for the rod against the wall

Tiptoeing out the back door to where the bicycle lay

Swiftly mounted with rod in hand and an intensity of purpose

The wheels turned rhythmically, reflecting the first blushes of sunlight against the rims

An orange ball gently caressed the horizon peering upwards to eternity

His breath condensed in the early morn air, forming a luminous fog flowing past his face

Rod rattling & birds chirping, mingling harmoniously with the dewy grassy haze

His bicycle swept gently through the winding countryside

Each revolution of the wheels heightening the anticipation

Daybreak transforming to light as the sun moved gracefully higher

Blinding colour above the tree tops, clouds dancing through the skies

Edging closer to the location that he'd dreamt of all night

Eventually, the dam came within sight and he pedaled even harder

Onwards ever faster, hedgerows and road drowned out by his breathing

Freedom, from school, family, friends, at one with himself and nature

Bike screeching to a halt, pebbles flying, resonating against the rusty gate

Steam rising from his warm clothing as he wiped the sweat from his face

Fingers, prised from the golden rod, which was gently placed against the railings

Hands moved swiftly to secure the bicycles lock, click and then the short walk to freedom

He danced through the glistening grass, each pace in tune with the music of the river

Feeling, seeing, hearing, at last he was immersed in the place of his dreams

Reaching the dam he was filled with apprehension, waiting to see her condition

Peering over the top, she flowed steadily treasuring her own secrets

Below in the river the strains of gentle sounds mixed metaphorically with natures own

Flies danced atop the dam, then spirited away higher, returning later rippling the glass

Announcing their arrival for those waiting to play

A gentle splash as a small salmon broke the surface, missing its prey

He swiftly descended the bank towards waters edge, moving downstream

That favourite spot beckoned, where low water caressed those smooth rocks

Rod was swiftly cast into the ebbing current and spinner splashed

Click, and the gentle reeling of line, waiting for that expectant tug

Over and over the pull of current, watching waiting viewing that line

Closer and closer she comes, as excitement wanes, waiting lustfully for that next cast

He became lulled by the magic of the river, flies circling in the sunlight

Diving against the water's surface as if to tease the fish below

Casting again visualizing that dream of first fish being fulfilled

Then reeling steadily, through the rippling flows, his senses were awakened

Rod bending swiftly and the feel of electricity as his arms tightened their grip

Excitement flowed through every pore of his body as his pulse raced

His mind was overcome with joy as the sensations filled him with emotion

Questioning, over and over, will she stay on the line till home

Expectation gave way to unbridled joy as she leapt upwards through water's surface

A small trout, but to him she was perfection

He continued to reel, but now at a quickening pace, withdrawing to rivers edge

She flickered through the shallows surrendering to the cool morning air and a grassy bank

His heartbeat quickened as he killed, her heart beat now gone forever

Visualization now fulfilled, he lay back on the wet grass absorbing the moment

Released momentarily from the river he looked upwards at the clouds

Brightly racing across the sky like puffs of smoke teasing each other

Blinding sunlight cascaded through as he glanced away, reflections

Wading through the cold waters of the river feale, dreaming the next dream.

Jessica Clark

Snow

Light and bright
and I am made a child again by snow,
something aglow inside,
re-lit embers,
today remembers
giddy exaltations of snow-days in school,
footprint paths stamped up Parliament Hill,
panting and dragging a home-made toboggan.
Breathless slide and tramping inside
to the warmth of hot chocolate,
pub choc-a-block of kids and mums and dads and dogs.
Mittens, scarves,
collecting clouds from the tops of cars,
in London it turned quickly into slush
and it's easy to push these memories away.
Melt into the mire of years,
until on the first day of February,
the sudden carpet of white takes you by surprise.
Less inclined to build snowmen now,

to play games hurling snowballs,

to lie and craft an angel...

Half of me feels somewhat inconvenienced,

by thoughts of how wet my shoes will get,

catching cold or being slowed en route somewhere,

will it frizz up my blow-dried hair?

But drawing back the curtains,

there's a gleam

of something only seen in those childhood escapes.

Rush of excitement because the world looks different,

like a nativity scene

or the inside of a globe.

And when the sun bounces off smoothed-out rooftops

I want to run and smell the alpine air

face lifted skywards

cheeks red and blushing with laughter,

soul discarding some learned grown-up heaviness.

White, white, purer than yesterday,

first ecstatic snowfall of the year.

Who knows how long it will stay –

So let's relish the way the morning dazzles,

rest awhile in that twinkling, softened joy,

set our footprints down before it fades.

Alison Liew

How Normal Feels Like

I lost count of the moon's passing and days

torn from an aging calendar's face

since our 'forever' became 'never', when I noticed the syllables

in the mirth dripping from my lips

as I danced behind glass walls of white-collared crowds

joined in the beat of Beatles - or

scorched by chamomile on rough tongue, forgetting

curses hurled at every wrong turn I took because I know

these detours can never lead me more astray than I once was.

My own person was a mystery, a stranger with alien habits

till I sat down with her in a tea party with pens for spoons

and cups of ink. We gouged valleys and canyons from the tales coursing through our veins, explored worlds trapped in

shelves and raced the wind to embrace sunsets. As we return home,

feet sore from miles of adventure I found a friend in my

shadow.

Rituals, they stitch the seams of reality -

first awakening my lungs and driving me out into the breeze

of gossiping trees and rush of glinting metal

heaving with slaves to society. Spared from such fate, I am not

but from the art surrounding my body comes forth a holy refuge

I seek devotedly.

This legacy of little victories,

saw battles won against invisible enemies,

humming ballads beloved by us without

breaking down like the leaves

uncurling on a humid night. Loud triumphant cries, you can hear

when I rejoice with dry sleeves and a skin

freed from blades.

Last but not least, I hold new memories -

icy pricks under a shared umbrella,

blending in with every shade of misfits living in the dark with light

in their eyes, and

pillow fights with a renegade behind a door of fire breathers and oracles.

Bizarre, yet these memories show me a new home to live in.

This journey of almost four seasons is far from over,

but I am not afraid anymore when I now know

how it feels like to be normal again.

Peter Donelly

Devon in my nineteenth year

You would think the autumn of 1998

changed my life, when I went to university.

In many ways it did,

but we must go back still further

to July of that year
when I stayed with my great-uncle and aunt.
Not my first time away from home,
but my first long journey out on my own.

They gave me gunpowder tea
for breakfast and for supper,
took me to see my great-grandma
for the final time,
to a theatre in Plymouth.
Over the Cornish border to Cotehele,
inland to Fingle Bridge and Castle Drogo,
to Dartmouth on my very last day.

Forgetting the past,
not fearing for the future,
in those clear moments, I couldn't help but wish
life could stand as still at its peak as
the photographs we took.

© *CHRISTINE BUTLER*

Motion

Norbert Góra

This is how the journey looks like

Clothed in thrill,
travelling again,
to a place where the eyes
can be amazed
and the brain will remember
a sequence of moments

(how many of them
will be remembered after years?)

Different air
falls into the mouth,
the senses feed
with a rush of unknown smells,
people, the same
(if not entirely).
time has to chase me now
to be able to write it
on the cards of life
constantly moving
from the future to the past,
through the present.

Darren Donohue

Grace

The knowing half-light of twilight -
half grief, half enchantment -

streams down on this Apple Green,
this petrol station I enter

in a state of grace. So long
holed up, nursing wounds,

nestled in morphine's velvet embrace,
I dream my way to a cushioned seat.

I find coffee-eyed couples
prodding their phones,

hatching uncertain futures.
I too am hatching,

breaking through. Like a new-born chick,
I fight my way into world.

You comb grey hair from my eyes,
and it settles, between renewal and decay.

James Swansbrough

Remember When

you run me up 27 in your daddy's '64 Sting Ray con-
vertible, the early
summer sun licking our arms and the wind popping
what hair couldn't fit our
hats. You were in a t-shirt and ripped jeans, frame-bent
Ray Bans veiling your
eyes. We lit out for Spring City and back.
You wore sandals that you'd kick off into the floor-
board so you could pad the
clutch barefoot, and I don't recall the color of your toe
polish but I'm sure it
was chipped from neglect because I started loving you
then for not being
always perfect and made up like a sorority girl.
And I know I wasn't the only man started loving you
that day, because you talked
torque, horse, and cubic inches to the handful of guys
admiring the car's curves at
the gas station, the lingo flowing so casually from you
it like to've ripped their

inseams. Then you broke their hearts:

They all died a little when your wrist flicked ignition,

that motor barking low, loud,

and dangerous as a Jonathan Edwards sermon, cursing

their ears with

unattainable salvation. Hallelujah hot damn. Gravel

crunched as the rubber made

asphalt and those 250 horses snorted and charged us

out city limits past Soddy to

Sale Creek, then Graysville, Dayton, Evensville, clear

to Watts Bar.

Past juke joints and dollar stores we hurtled, around

bends and roadside memorials,

brokedown cars and trucks in need of a spare—tire,

fuel pump, lifetime. On through

towns with more churches than traffic signals, with

boarded up businesses and

foreclosed homes dotting their landscape, riverside

boat ramps the only free place for a good time.

We piped country music and hair metal over that rum-

bling din, discussing favorite

tunes, not knowing then we heard the first song we'd
dance to as a married couple.
Wish I'd known where we were when it hit the radio.
I'd place my own wreath off
the shoulder, leave it to sunbleach and weather the ex-
haust of other vehicles, their
occupants heedless or indifferent, but needing it—
A memorial to something found rather than lost,
merged instead of
torn apart. Long-lasting. And us miles and lifetimes
away from then—but
together, burning down new roads.

Zoe Ellesmore

Driving, on the South Circular

You and me. Stuck in traffic half
way to the hospital. That bloody road.
You in the driver's seat, me
an origami fold next to you, waiting

for the lights to change.
Keep breathing.

In for four out for eight. Breathing
through the weight of her, half
way between my womb and world. Changing
shapes—I'm a rainbow, a reef knot. I focus on the
road,
on the blinking red stars of waiting
cars counting each breath back to me.

Soon it won't just be me
and you, breathing.
Nine months testing, worrying, waiting
for a life to grow, here in half
a moonlit night.   The road
    false starts - lights change

green, change
                                back   red
again. Foul mouthed me,
growling at the road.
Keep breathing
through the windswept days, the half

slept nights, the weigh-in waiting

rooms, the ancient rhymes. Waiting
for her bluebird eyes to change
to my old sparrow brown. The hint of a half
smile. A laugh. In my nightdress soaked with milk,
as the sun slips down, breathing
on the window glass, watching the road

for you. Crossing the road,
holding tight, waving off, waiting
for her to come home. Keep breathing.
Change
is good you tell me.
But sometimes I'm half scared. Half

a life lived. The second half
about to begin. Her, you and me
on the road, breathing, waiting for the lights to
change.

Nathanael O'Reilly

Reprieve

At twelve twenty-five on a Saturday
I walk east in my laceless Converse
from the Discount Tire store on the I-20
frontage road, my bank balance four-
hundred and ninety dollars lower, uphill
through the vacant lot, climb over rocks,
step around cactus through dry brown
grass past empty thirty-two-ounce Styrofoam
Whataburger cups, a prone For Lease sign
and tangles of Texas barbed wire, through
the strip mall parking lot by Mattress Firm,
the Cotton Patch Café and Great Clips,
across expanses of cracked concrete baking
in ninety-seven-degree heat to the Starbucks
on South Main, seeking iced coffee, Siggi's
Icelandic skyr, a reprieve from Texas
summer heat and a quiet place to read
poetry, listen to Pearl Jam, peruse the latest
report on the India v. England test match,
check email, scroll through Facebook, Instagram
and Twitter, catch up on the lives of family,

friends, colleagues and strangers

while bearded, tattooed workers in grey

shorts, shirts and caps install four new tires.

Bernadette Jameson

Traffic Flow

Streams of white headlights race to the city,

empty stars or supernovae

move toward the heart's beating chambers.

Trails of red lights in outbound arteries,

blood plumping fingertips,

a million oxygenated cells bringing the life home.

I see them through the fogged-up windows on a bus,

in the darkness on a bridge—I could be anywhere;

spending more time than I can spare.

Stopping to let on and out.

Exchanging gasses, red turns blue.

empty bus at the night's last stop, leaving behind forgotten gloves.

© *CHRISTINE BUTLER*

Reflections

John Carew

Tonight is for my Odyssey

On a frosty moonlit night

Strong boots, warm coat, and woolly hat, I take a walk

Grass crisp and white under foot

I come to a stone wall, stiled to cross

Think of the men who built this wall

Hands placing stone carefully upon stone

Their names forgotten, this their only legacy

Then, the oak tree

Denuded of its leaves in its deep winter's sleep

Waiting for spring and for the life-giving sap to flow through its veins

Bringing new growth to its branches

Next, the old graveyard

Not one of orderly rows. Here souls are buried wherever possible

Headstones, mossed and whitened from time and weather.

I run my fingers over an engraving

    Josephine O'Brien nee Murphy

    1901 – 1946

    Her son Patrick, 1926 -1928

Eighteen years - was she waiting for the day she'd

reunite with him?

I leave the graveyard with a prayer

Walk on to a church

Stained glass windows and a bell tower illuminated by the

Moon's light

I cannot enter, but I know it well

St Patrick, Jesus, Stations of the Cross, and its confes-
sionals

the Blessed Virgin—all are statues

The smiles and tears of family

Neighbours and of friends, held within these holy
walls

A prayer for my children at my father's grave, "may
they be safe

and happy all their lives"

Jump the wall into the school yard

The playful sounds of children swilling in the air

I think of my years here as a boy

Illuminating of - a simpler time

Wandering to my mother's house

Light in her window. Do I visit her?

No, not tonight. Tonight is for my odyssey

Leave this old woman, whom I love

To her rosary and knitting

Still, onwards to the fields of youth

Where we played games intense as any all-Ireland se-
nior final

Brothers, sisters, cousins, calling names out in the summer evenings

Of our heroes

but a memory now

until I reach the rock that was,

In penal days, a lookout for the Redcoats as

mass and prayers were uttered

To An Teampall Nua

A place that holds remains of many souls, including

Thomas O'Connellan

> Dear Molly St. George
>
> Is a maid without peer
>
> So handsome, so modest
>
> So graceful, so dear

across the waters of Loughgur

Dark and broody,

Gearóid Iarla on his white steed, the Bean an 'ti' brushing her long

hair with a golden comb

Were I that buachaill, would I want that comb for my-self?

Cold moves me on

and to the Giant's Grave

A wedge tomb from the old Stone Age

A sacred place to bury the dead

With food and drink for their passage to another world

And, half an hour's passing brings me to a circle of stones

Built by the Neolithic Bronze-Age man

A place of ritual, a site to honour gods

Aligned to the sunrise of the summer Solstice

These people, the engineers of their time

I stand - in awe of them -

Soon the dawn will break

Niamh O 'Meara

Reminiscence

How charming, life beneath the spindle boughs
looks to me now.
Like a Monet - I have painted it prettier than
it might have been.
And here I am, standing in the desert.
Suffocating slowly,
in a wide, open space.
Because I am alone, and away from the tribe who knew
me,
when I was just a child.
There's a warm breeze that shakes these ghost gums,
their branches poised like a corporal's gun.
A pretty sight, beneath a night sky laden with stars.
But I am weighted down—down by the pull of my own
roots.

Kat Dyb

Time Zones

We used to think of airports as storages of lost

memories. Muted sounds of other people's destina-
tions

we will never discover. Maybe we do not have to journey

anymore, you taught me the in-betweens.

Nearby sleeps someone I do not love and far away

sleeps the someone I love - in these margins un-
touched

by the distance. If we have to talk about love

then I prefer the shorter space between

two sides of the bed. Crossing it, we will press soft
lines

on a bed sheet, a forever changing map.

How much of what we call, from the lack of a better
definition,

love, can fit between the time zones?

Ruby McCann

I'm still considering

I'm still considering

beginnings..,

...so pleased to hear you
I like bright and dark sounds
that saxophone   screams
something lonesome

I'm new here
re-new-ed   been before
was born here   re-turn-er
it's like locking a woman in a room
with an angry man

feels alright   now
in this moment...
...he's on the right side of angry
lonely won't leave him alone
and this place stinks to high heavens
doesn't that tell you something?

don't know what's ahead
I've lost my sea legs

yes   the ocean   I'm here
at the Firth of Clyde
flowing into the Atlantic
to you   my dear friend
on the other side
its daunting sometimes
the vast infinite width
and depth   the divide

other times
it un-anchors me
takes me down deep within
a-minor tsunami at low tide

calms too   calming   yes
yes   calm as the day
Icarus fell chasing dreams

was he fallen?   did he fall?
smashed against a rock
I heard   seas
unpredictable like that
a sudden change in weather

raging surfs slap like angry parents
my mother   once
not my father   shocked me
she cried afterwards   empty-eyed
like a ghost in the kitchen

me too   silently
alone in the bathroom
knowing   I deserved it

I know these are small things
just coasting   not just
still there are days I feel I can't be fussed
I know I need to re-adjust
re-learn to trust
get real   or completely combust
then I turn like tides

today the flow can't wait
cause it's so good to hear from you
whitecaps rolling in
my lips curling   a-drifting smile
softening   splaying

foaming high-pitched
strains on that horn   whispering

s'bin too long

I catch you on the high note
I'm switched on   enriched
screaming staccato   you got me bewitched
releasing water keys
it's been a long session
sliding cross rhythms
my trans-Atlantic connection

Jen   Nolan

Rest

With brighter step and quickened pace
I turned from stressful daily grind
To visit the old quiet place
And left the heavy days behind

I've laboured many miles to be

now shrouded in the quiet air
Watching dozy bumblebees
Bobbing here and buzzing there

The flowers bloom in pinks and blues
Blanket-thick across the fields
They paint the world bright with their hues
And to this sight my sorrows yield

The crowds in steeples tall and grey
Say words that cut and settle deep
In bones and heart as soft as clay
They tell me joy's not mine to keep.

A mattress soft beneath the moon
Counting stars and fireflies
Peace creeps back slowly, none too soon
As dawn paints pinks across the skies

The sun is gold and warm and strong
As I skip stones across the lake
I think I've known it all along
My joy was never theirs to take

Jessica Clark

Days of yore

I see your withered skin and deafened ears
while opening for you our kitchen door
but I don't see your growth across the years.

Aided by old care-home volunteers,
we take your coat, your handbag on the floor,
 and sit you down – the tea-time hour nears.

Though maybe you expose my inner fears
of bathing in the glow of youth no more,
I listen as the conversation steers

to things you've done and how you spent your years,
jobs abroad and growing up through the War,
the tea is poured as all the table hears...

and in my soul there suddenly appears
a sense of life in those old days of yore;

and in your words, the dust between us clears.

In these tales from before, there disappears
my prejudice – I look at you in awe,
and see in your eyes the wisdom of lived years
beyond your withered skin and deafened ears.

Ella Taylor

The Redwoods

Each has a journey to the sky to reach the light, to feel the sun touching the face of each leaf, each branch and twig. How wide, how high, how long have they been alive? Each trunk is joined by their roots in the same soil.

The Redwoods of Rhinefield are alive. And this pair of giants stretch 50 metres high, joining the grass to the sky. To hold them, is to embrace that which has lived through war

and ruin. To hold them, is

to touch a past still rooted in the forest that I see to-day. 160 years and still growing,

reaching for the warmth of the sun.

The forest is ever changing yet remaining, as the world beyond the treeline goes to

sleep and then begins again. The roots hold firm and the trees bend as the breeze blows away the debris.

Weathered to show every fault and every curve of the trunk, the Redwoods wear their skin like the face of those who lived in the pursuit of love and sacrifice. Roots gripping the ground as

leaves fall in the autumn.

homecoming

Amber

Anne Hornsby

The Wanderer's Return

Doors open wide, like an embrace.
The plants on the porch
seemed to point me inside.

I stepped in, to the delicious smell
of my Mother's baking,
All would be well.
The vibrant patterns of the carpet on the floor leapt
Out at me; I noticed them more,
having been away a while.

My Mother was waiting.

On her tired face, a welcoming smile

My Father followed me in,

Complaining about the weight of my rucksack,

He put it down asking, how I could have carried that,

All around Europe, on my little back?

Sunlight spilled in through the blinds.

The settee swallowed me

in all its old familiarity.

The sound of the radio,

Of china cups on saucers,

Of my Dad calling me

His favourite daughter

I sit back,

Inhale deeply,

let the tension unravel

After all my travels

It was good to be home.

Ruby McCann

Homespun

odyssey-ing like Grange Copeland
thought family gave hope
man
said: societal trope man
ain't personal..,

...well
left disappointed
everything's disjointed..,
...flip side on this third life
fire burns within

no brimstone   like Lot's wife
pillar of salt   spilling strife   delivered by angels

say what?

loops around incessantly
drowning in fusion-ed revelry
attempting balancing backwards

altering   moving forward

floating   round and round

this drifting crescendo

rebounding   reedy   gentle

hollow sparks of blues imbue the air

he's set in a cold sweat

clasping a bass   clarinet

dude's dead-set

on cracking sound

thoughts close to breaking

intentionally participating

appropriating a Clockwork

Orange   fluid interlude

he's squeezing laid back tempo

exhaling earthy sighs

releasing high-pitched sound

freeing fusions   improvised

bars and measures crash   mesmerising mellow

harsh dark beats   burst   very temperamen-
tal

bird song fades   in and out   drifting transcenden-
tal

lost in unchartered territory   he's screeching instru-
mental

muffled   muted   breathless

getting very restless

somewhere in the interval

between two notes

moving through the backwoods

carrying only packed goods

mouth-piece-ing   melodies

back-dropped   childhood memories

appease

tensions ease

Anne Hornsby

Coming Home

My Mother used to say

"It's nice to have a holiday,

but it's nice to come back home again".

I used to mutter

I'd rather have stayed away

And had another holiday.

Coming home -

A return to the familiar

Everything in its place

Routine

Nothing unexpected

Claustrophobic

Suffocating

Enclosing

I longed to open my soul

Tear down the walls

Expose new places

Experiences

I longed for a distant, larger goal.

SHIFTING   HORIZON   ©   JOAN
FULLERTON

Expanse

Geno Naughton

Robinsonade

Bent and beat on the ale-foam breakers,

Lord, he was a distant man,

Hemmed in by sea circling all around,

A beaming down sun on some remote stretch

Flustering him. Sternly awaiting the taps to be pulled

For ruby-hewed fury in a stout standing glass,

Schooner size, on the rocks, clad with an unruly head
-

On his shoulders near shore-corals and the hermit shell-house.

The dust-sand is whiter now in twelve o'clock lights.

The sun goes down on him and the gulls,

Bathing reality under a level Pacific

Where every horizon looks that bit less real

Than the last. One true dusk. Skimming stones
Because it's easier than accepting truth.
Shorelines and jawlines morph into one
Caustic imagery of peoples and things. Obsolete
With perfect detachment he sits dizzied
In a brew-trance, reaching further into memory's
Eye at high-tide in seasick noons. Gone afar
Gathering sea glass from crystalline floors,
Every bottle giving abundant confirmation.

Ross Walsh

An Galar Mór

Loose coins jingle in my
pocket, everything I
own on my back. Lining
up to board the metal
coffin ship and flee. Flee
across the world, tracing

the journey of all those
before me in reverse.
While they were thrashed by cold

angry waves, I will

sail amongst the stars and

hope the coughing does not

follow me. They left be-

-hind the peat bogs and the

oak forests and fields of

green grass, white snowdrops and

orange barley. They came

for Lady Liberty,

embracing their huddled

masses. I leave behind

the steel and concrete of

the city, rising up

and up to pierce the sky

and point accusingly

at God. I head towards

the faerie rings of home,

the quiet wailing of

a banshee in the wind,

a call to prepare an-

-other coffin. Before,

they ran from Famine, An
Gorta Mór. Now I find
myself fleeing, homeward
bound, from Pestilence, An
Galar Mór. Another
horseman coming for us.

Converge

Stephanie Hanson

Old Town

Winnowing away, ripples of immeasurable pain are lost
One after the other,

While we, under the sun, consume dipped colours.

Lashes of pure light, settling into streams, filter down,

Bathing the dozy town in cool brightness

People trickle in and out of streets

Our feet begin to peter out the prints of other's paths
like cresting waves over scratches in the sand

Walking further, we encounter

The Old Town:

Windows replaced with boarded hollows,

City buildings dyed full red, once immaculate

Now drifted to a shade of pale sockeye

Walls, laced with spools of steel barbed wire where

Paint reels backwards to reveal the naked brick

We recollect

Asking ourselves,

Who left their boots behind?

Time washes over

Children, Mothers and their Sons

Somewhere between.

Through cracks,

Shoots start to recover empty space

As Seasons

Chip, chip, chip away at blinding horror -
slow, like turning leaves

Danielle Silverman

Snout of the Year

You turn on a podcast about rhinology
before
We lay down
On the purple throws on
The floor.

For eight years
We slept toe
To snout
Underneath the glow
Of a shrinking Christmas tree.

Our yearly ritual:
To come to this house,
The impression of a fading memory,
Sometimes forgetting
How long we have been

Here.

The rooms keep
Moving further
Away.

We cook the thin slices of
Marbled meat,
Throw in white strings of
Enoki mushrooms,
And watch as yellow puffs of
Tofu bob on the boiling
Broth.

What's there to mourn but
The lifetimes ahead of us.
Like soft pearls on an
Aging string,
We desperately reach to
Hold each other close.
To remain taut.

"You know how I know what rhinology is?"

"How?"

"There was a city in ancient Egypt I read about called
Oxyrhynchus.

Town of the sharp-snouted fish."

But you already drift asleep,

Somewhere between

Sharp and

Fish.

Kevin Griffin

What the Wall Said

You brought your eyes

filled with unused tears

to rest your elbows here,

become part of serenity

ease into history

see the smiling stones,

the greying cement,

now giving the calm

you didn't know you needed.

I am the wall, the sum
of more than what made me.

Call on a substitute soul,
make a roll call of the plants,
mint... here, camomile...present,
moss...all over, ivy...coming,
foxglove ... foxglove... struggling, Sir,
pennywort...right here, hart's tongue...busy,
rockcress... grass...the fungi.
All here.

The breeze from the West and South
brings an alien cold,
returning yesterday's bitterness
that came from the East.

Holly Parkinson

St. John's Street

You welcome us with open arms

Aside tumultuous past

With grandeur and with rays of gold
A home for us, at last.

May we slip between your buildings
May your passage take our feet
In vain you sapped from nectar but
She came back, twice as sweet.

Remember what you taught us
Like a goddess taught before:
I do not do, I do not do,
as you do, anymore.

Elijah MacBean

Bridge

I don't know if it was all a dream,
If I ever really left this room.
If I travelled through oceans with my eyes closed and
my tray table down.

Where you pay for Coca-Cola with paper and not
coins.

One day I just woke up back in my mother's house again like I was a child,

With these vivid stories of new ceilings and humidity.

But every memory is singular,

And the extras are stood inverted

Walking on the wrong side of the road.

There's no phone numbers or names,

And the only part that makes sense is standing in that precise section of the Chattahoochee Riverwalk bridge that has unclarity.

The part where you don't know if you're an hour ahead of behind,

In Alabama or Georgia.

That's the only part that feels real.

© *CHRISTINE BUTLER*

Hollow

Aldo Quagliotti

Meta-morphosis

I know that my future does not translate
into peaking, nor into ministerial codes
pregnancy doesn't fall straight
into bilateral jurisdiction
future is way off-track
when you're modelling your own shape
bright-eyed determination coasts
the abysmal call of depression

I have a perilous affinity
for darkness crowding in
spreading unsafely
through my prosopagnosia:
I recognize the mirage-like face
the whimsy trait d'union:

a mother is a map
a father is the compass

I'm the tracing
of a hundred people
of both
of nobody
I'm the question mark
never the answer

Asha Sumroy

Meditations on an Empty House

We are written onto these walls
And our love lingers between them

We etched our names into the plaster, wood, the bath-
rooms, bedrooms, bed frames and doors in permanent
pen ink

Markers as strong as the Tubi 60

Back of the throat burning

Israeli shots we learnt to love in the bar beneath stone
arches

To make sure who ever lived here after us would know
that we were here, that

We learnt each other's lives

each other's bodies here

It was here in this room on a warm night in May that
you became my family,

At this table, too small for us all to sit around without
sticking unwashed thighs together we shared food like
sharing ourselves

In this bathroom we sang out of tune duets to wake
our souls in the morning, taking

Turns with the shampoo

Tossing it between shower curtains

On these sofas we administered wine to cope with
2017's election, projected onto

These walls from England - two hours behind and
nothing near what we know of home now

This bookshelf shared our favourite stories, aside
worn-cornered manifestos

This bed we shared the nights we needed to be held

The nights we needed to, we fought

Then tore up the tears with laughter and, eventually,

Song

It's strange to return to an empty house.

The signatures we left to mark memory territory are
just one generation of graffiti

The family after us have been and gone and left their
narrative in the space between ours and the hole one of
them must have kicked through the kitchen wall

I kept my key

in the hope I'd come back and find you all sat in your
bedrooms

We are written onto these walls

We wrote ourselves there to preserve our love between
them

But continents divide

Our marks are

just a background to the hologram memories that are bringing me to tears

I know we walked this floor, I'm sure that I can see the footprints

mapped in the dirt we forgot to clean

We cigarette-burnt ourselves into the plastic chairs on this balcony

I can see the smoke leaving your lips

That hair wound up onto the shower wall

I swear

even years on it must be one of yours and I convinced myself

that someone else's unwashed sheets

smelt of us

Here, we spoke and lived in revolution

I kept my key so I could come back to find it

But here I am alone, sat in an empty house

With all of our names scribbled

in ink fading on the walls

Danielle Silverman

Tory Cave

And I who served
the King of England,
Now hide as
Jacob Salisbury,
Found cold which forced my refuge
was the warmth that led
All Helderberg's Patriots to me.
Like some cruel grey deluge,
Was smoke in the cavern's chimney,
that decried expiation for what homes
I blackened myself.

A thick moss on the lintel.
A camouflage of foliage,
Ferns *kiss* among the slate.
But it's not enough for
Another tomorrow.

When they find me here,
When tried and hung,
My prayer on my
tongue.
Begs to be between stone
Pillars,
and those ancient
molluscan souls,
embedded in the walls
which consoled me in the
dark.
some silent
dripping   falling
into
little pools,
echoing
Mohawk and
Mohegan cries,
Whispering-
I was not the first,
nor the last.

And will they know my name,

From my *loyalties*?

Or will it dissipate?

If strung

from the roof of this void

the body becoming

Speleothemic

peaceful

hanging,

perhaps one perseveres,

assuming

Something older,

Something more.

It's too late to

change loyalties.

too late to crawl

deeper into the womb

of dust and stone.

too late to believe in anything

but the last two leaves on

tufted pussy willow.

or the moonlight outside.

or the silent wings

of hawks

passing

over.

Jessica Clark

Cleaning out the fridge

(Based on true events)

It seems a shame to dispose of mould formed in such intricate constellations,

And clearly for some time no one else has felt the obligation:
What is this orange gunk and why is it partially blue?

Near the front, everything's new,

vegetables innocent and edible.

But do not go gentle into that student fridge,
Where old green beans have found a way to leak and divisions into individual produce are a long-extinct system;
Between repetitions of pasta sauces,

Only the eye divorces landfill waste from that retaining taste.

This clean-out is a game, a ritual,

though not frequent enough to be habitual,

a vigil for fruits and legumes only half-consumed,
now doomed to be eroded by curious multiplying life
forms,
into a fluid of no colour that films the shelves and
sticks to packets and cans of beer.

Beware the humous tub, my son,

Beware its pinkish dots and shun

The softened pepper with its grey-black bruise.
How much booze and garlic and cheese and reduced
price tomatoes has this fridge known prior to our
own?
What tenants before ourselves were here?

I see myself years from now

In some version of the British Dream:

No white picket fence but a set of perfectly-matching
teacups, evenings tuning into the BBC and 2.4 children.
Our fridge will be spotless, rotless, at least certainly
not this allotment of micro-life with enough variety to
rival one of the science site's labs.

But there's so little left of my student years

that these findings bring no tears

yet somehow endear me to the nest we shared shelter
in awhile.

I may one day with hindsight smile at the messy chaos
that allowed such mould to flourish,

growths that we let seed while swapping stories in the
kitchen
doubling in fits of laughter

or confiding our fears.

Thus, the motion and emotion of student chaos left no
time   for   the   depths   of   our   refrigerator.
These constellations in green are to me no less obscene
than the world outside,

whose doors we're soon to swing through –

long behind this family of fungal spores,

No weirder than stars from whom we take our wisdom.

I scrape it to the bin with a grimace,

mop at the muck,

while at the edges of my vision, the future glimmers.

Will we always be like this? Joking, hoping, dreaming

and bitching.

Stop overthinking, and clean up the kitchen.

Pete Chambers

Nearly There

Truck depot on industrial estate,

    the day before the day before Christmas Day

        and I'm looking my age.

       Train window stark reflections,

            end of the decade. Self inspec-
            tion.

       Hands are calloused.

              Eyes. Dark hollow

       An empty carriage moving through
       time

              as decorations glint
              are left behind

     left behind.

        Cold wet fields.

All of England in the night,

     and if you can't step into the same river
     twice

        I will fix it in memory.

        The girl in trainer.

Southampton docks.

     Shipping containers.

           Rotten pontoons.

My Dad's Dad worked here a long time ago and

        when he was 6 or so years old

          watched the Titanic put out for America

But the Titanic sank

      and my Grandad died before I was born, killed

        by the filfthy, miserable work of the poor.

Silicosis. Oxygen tanks. Christmas tress in the windows of flats.

    Topps Tiles. Rain light on Aldi. Taxi drivers waiting on standby.

      Stars now and then, no moon. Plenty booze.

        48 percent to 52.

      'Merry Christmas and a Happy New Year'.

Cool

Obinna Chilekezi

Early Morning Rain

(Banjul, 23/09/18)

It rained heavily this morning
With showers, strong winds and sandstorm
The wind with big strong hands shaking everything
At sight. There I perched.
It rained,
And a bird in its apartment drenched continued
to sing sweet songs in the rain
Sweet birdly songs - even in that heavy morning rain!

Alice Carlill

saltwater

there is something about the point
where the land
meets the sea,
a dissolve
where substance
gives way.
the edges of things
are there
& not
just like
my reflection
in the rock pools -
silted silver on the shore.

it is funny
to find
you know yourself

only
by way
of not knowing -
of seeing
by not seeing.

but that's how
boundaries
work
I suppose.

is it not?

& look,
there's the moon
full luminescence
outliving
the clichés
& the hillocks of pebbles
undulating down
towards the fetid seaweed
seeping its particular
ripe, alive smell.

there are gulls cawing
overhead
battering crab corpses
onto the stony floor
indifferent to my presence.

that's the thing -

despite the fact
that my body
in this landscape
bears no weight
leaves no trace
washed away
by tomorrow's tide -
despite the fact
that it does not
need me
to be -

this is where I most am.

Harry   Mizumoto

a complex system of weights and pulleys

The fragility of a train in rain
an image tending to flicker out
The fragility of a small, sullen boy
pulling taut the edge of his green shirt
The cut between pant and sneaker / a bone
showing through flesh / the strain of skin over it
body / to hand / to finger / suspended against
wrinkled plastic
a tongue slick against roof / a slow glide of eyelid
A woman / her eyes and nose and mouth / so far apart
smiles
the way a flower blooms: by peeling
each petal tenderly apart from its center

Cameron   Bramley

Shimmer

As I look over the
oceans of my sunsets

my mind wanders to hazy green.

out there the waves alone slow.

They crack the rocks and shore as if

guided to fight the earth.

People bask in my surroundings,

the deep, bold war-like sun captures everything

The ripples of the ocean now darker with

light

Meander, ripping into somewhere.

as i sit here in awe of God's country,

I hold my arms high as if to grab the sky,

pull the sun down deeper into the cold

stone of my heart.

I too have been a shoreline,

battered by the waves of life,

Gasped for air,

Fought to breathe

cried,

shivered of cold,

burnt by the very sun I adore—

the sunset over my ocean

A wonderful paradox.

I am lifted.

Gareth Writer-Davies

Here

should I come into money

I won't
travel

I've only just got
here

to gamble
home
against a sweeping view of paradise
islands under an azure sky

is risky
as one grows older and walking home at
dusk thoughts
turn

to how time passes

like an unsought obligation to the unfound
and unseen

and to pack one's belongings in a case and
fly seems an awful bother
a flimsy sort of dream

here
I will cease my roving and stay the
knowing eye

grow familiar
and watch the world go by

Acknowledgment

A heartfelt thank you to each of our contributing poets, whose unique perspectives have paved our own journey through the editorial process of this collection.

Our deepest gratitude goes to Joan Fullerton and Christine Butler, whose dazzling art brings colour and sophistication into these pages.

Credits

Aaronson, Veronica 'Leaving Iona – North Beach'
Bramely, Cameron, 'Dive into Darkness'
——— 'Desert Rose'
——— 'Shimmer'
Brown, Abi, 'Torrent'
Butler, Janet, 'Childhood'
——— 'Vanishing Point'
Byrne, Paul W., 'Fealeings'
Carew, John, 'The Atlas'
——— 'Tonight is for my Odyssey'
Carlill, Alice, 'saltwater'
Carr, Jennifer, 'A Prayer for My Owl Spirit'
——— 'In this Moment'
——— 'My Sanctuary'
Chambers, Pete, 'Nearly There'
Chilekezi, Obinna, 'Early Morning Rain'

—— 'I have to leave (a poem)'
Clark, Jessica, 'A story about a boat-trip'
—— 'Cleaning out the fridge'
—— 'Days of yore'
—— 'Snow'
Cushing, Bill, 'At a Mountain Waterfall'
Del Mundo, David, 'Barcafoba'
Donelly, Peter, 'Devon in my nineteenth year'
Donohue, Darren, 'Grace'
—— 'Postcard'.
—— 'Wanderlust'
Dyb, Kat, 'Time Zones'
Ellesmore, Zoe, 'Driving, on the South Circular'
Góra, Norbert, 'This is how the journey looks like'
Griffin, Kevin, 'What the Wall Said'
Halperin, Richard W., 'Prelude'
Hanson, Stephanie, 'Heat'
—— 'Old Town'
—— 'Plaza de Oriente'
Hornsby, Anne, 'Coming Home'
—— 'The Wanderer's Return'
—— 'Venice'
Jameson, Bernadette, 'Traffic Flow'
Khalyako, Tatiana, 'Wait for Me'
Liew, Alison, 'How Normal Feels Like'
MacBean, Elijah, 'Bridge'
McCann, Ruby, 'Homespun'

——— 'I'm still considering'

——— 'Ode to a Latin Stranger'

Mcevoy, Katie, 'Forever'

Mercieca, Daniel, 'Falcon'

Mhor, Bruach, 'In my top pocket—all the way'

Mizumoto, Harry, 'a complex system of weights and pulleys'

Mullen, Paul Robert, 'the journey'

Naughton, Geno, 'Robinsonade'

Newmark, Josh, 'Peace'

Nolan, Jen, 'Rest'

O 'Meara, Niamh, 'Reminiscence'

O'Reilly, Nathanael, 'Reprieve'

Parkinson, Holly, 'St. John's Street'

Proudfoot, Rose, 'Froglet'

Quagliotti, Aldo, 'Meta-morphosis'

Silverman, Danielle, 'Snout of the Year'

——— 'Tory Cave'

Smith, Richard, 'A New Dawn'

Sumroy, Asha, 'Desert Sun'

——— 'Meditations on an Empty House'

Swansbrough, James, 'Remember When'

Taylor, Ella, 'The Redwoods'

Walsh, Ross, 'An Galar Mór'

Writer-Davies, Gareth, 'Here'

Zee, Jakey, 'Choose Life'

All poems printed with the permission of the author.

Printed in Great Britain
by Amazon